Words to Know Before You Read

branch

chirped

feather

harming

nailing

nest

painted

piece

sawing

together

www.rourkeeducationalmedia.com

Edited by Precious McKenzie
Illustrated by Helen Poole
Art Direction and Page Layout by Renee Brady

Library of Congress PCN Data

The Birdhouse That Jack Built / Meg Greve
ISBN 978-1-61810-167-9 (hard cover) (alk. paper)
ISBN 978-1-61810-300-0 (soft cover)
Library of Congress Control Number: 2012936769

Also Available as:

*Scan for Related Titles
and Teacher Resources*

Rourke Educational Media
Printed in China, Artwood Press Limited,
  Shenzhen, China

rourkeeducationalmedia.com

customerservice@rourkeeducationalmedia.com • PO Box 643328 Vero Beach, Florida 32964

The Birdhouse That Jack Built

By Meg Greve

Illustrated by Helen Poole

This is the birdhouse that Jack built.

This is the nest on the ground that
fell from the branch without a sound.

The babies chirped and were sad. Jack said, "Don't worry! I will go get Brad!"

This is Brad who is good at art and drew the birdhouse to do his part.

by Brad

by Brad

Birdhouse design

hanger

wood

birds go in here

by Brad 11

This is Jack's friend who is really good at sawing and nailing a big piece of wood.

This is the painter who knew what to do. He painted the birdhouse a beautiful blue.

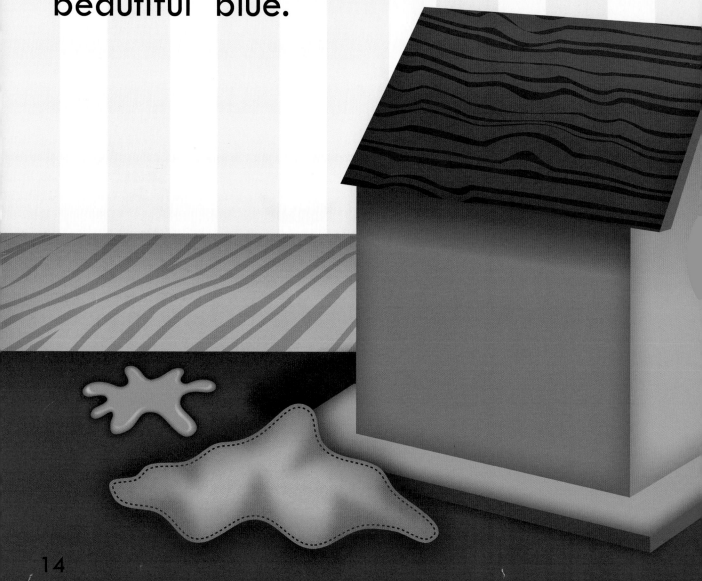

These are the friends who worked together to save some birds without harming a feather.

They drew and they sawed. They pounded and they painted.

18

This is the birdhouse they ALL built!

After Reading Activities

You and the Story...

Why did Jack want to build a birdhouse?

Describe, in order, how the friends built the birdhouse.

What lesson did you learn from this story?

Words You Know Now...

Make flashcards with the words from the story. Use index cards or cut up paper into cards. On one side, write the word. On the other side, write what the word means or draw a picture. Practice the words with a friend.

branch	nailing	sawing
chirped	nest	together
feather	painted	
harming	piece	

You Could...Build Your Own Bird Feeder!

You Will Need:
- one pine cone
- some birdseed
- peanut butter
- a piece of string or yarn
- one spoon or butter knife (ask an adult to help you)

What to Do:
1. Tie the string to the pine cone.
2. Using the spoon or butter knife, spread a generous amount of peanut butter all around the pine cone.
3. Roll the pine cone in bird seeds.
4. Hang the bird feeder in a tree you can see. Watch your happy bird friends come for a snack!

About the Author

Meg Greve lives in Chicago with her husband, daughter, and son. They have many birdhouses and bird feeders that they built together hanging in their backyard.

Meet The Author!
www.meetREMauthors.com

About the Illustrator

Helen Poole lives in Liverpool, England, with her fiancé. Over the past ten years she has worked as a designer and illustrator on books, toys, and games for many stores and publishers worldwide. Her favorite part of illustrating is character development. She loves creating fun, whimsical worlds with bright, vibrant colors. She gets her inspiration from everyday life and has her sketchbook with her at all times as inspiration often strikes in the unlikeliest of places!